BRITISH COLONIES on the Continent of NORTH AMERICA in about 1770 (with some notes)

New France until 1763, afterward British lands called Quebec and later called Canada

New France, called Louisianna until 1762, afterward Spanish lands called Spanish Louisianna

New Orleans, part of France until 1762, afterward part of Spain

New Spain until 1763, afterward British lands called West and East Florida

land claimed by South Carolina and by Georgia

Lake Huron

Lake Ontario

Lake Erie

Detroit

land claimed by Connecticut

Ohio R.

Wabash R.

Mississippi R.

Montreal

Quebec

St. Lawrence R.

NEW YORK

Albany

NEW HAMPSHIRE

MASSACHUSETTS

Falmouth later called Portland

Portsmouth

Charlestown & Cambridge

Concord and Lexington

Boston

MASSACHUSETTS

Plymouth

Hartford

RHODE ISLAND

Newport

Providence

New London

New York

Brooklyn

CONNECTICUT

Morristown

Valley Forge

Trenton

NEW JERSEY

PENNSYLVANIA

Philadelphia

Susquehanna R.

Delaware R.

Wilmington

DELAWARE

Baltimore

Annapolis

Potomac R.

Mount Vernon

MARYLAND

VIRGINIA

Richmond

James R.

Williamsburg

Yorktown

Norfolk

Roanoke R.

Cape Fear R.

NORTH CAROLINA

New Bern

Wilmington

Camden

SOUTH CAROLINA

Santee R.

GEORGIA

Savannah R.

Charleston

Altamaha R.

Savannah

Saint Augustine

ATLANTIC OCEAN

A Revolutionary
FiELD TRiP

Poems of   Colonial America

poems by *Susan Katz*   pictures by *R. W. Alley*

Simon & Schuster Books for Young Readers

New York   London   Toronto   Sydney

For Page and Jeff Hartling, who are a treasured part of my own history—S. K.

For Robert Gray, who taught me to believe in history—R. W. A.

For advice and assistance, the author wishes to thank:

Carla J. S. Messinger, retired executive director, Museum of Indian Culture, Allentown, Pennsylvania, and Grace Dove Ostrum, Lenape storyteller

SIMON & SCHUSTER BOOKS FOR YOUNG READERS
An imprint of Simon & Schuster Children's Publishing Division
1230 Avenue of the Americas, New York, New York 10020
Text copyright © 2004 by Susan Katz
Illustrations copyright © 2004 by R. W. Alley
All rights reserved, including the right of reproduction in whole or in part in any form.
SIMON & SCHUSTER BOOKS FOR YOUNG READERS is a trademark of Simon & Schuster, Inc.
Book design by Greg Stadnyk
The text for this book is set in 18-point Geometric 415.
The illustrations for this book are rendered in watercolor.
Manufactured in China
2 4 6 8 10 9 7 5 3 1
Library of Congress Cataloging-in-Publication Data
Katz, Susan.
A Revolutionary Field Trip : poems of colonial America / Susan Katz ; illustrated by R. W. Alley.
p. cm.
Summary: Twenty poems reveal life in colonial America as seen through the eyes of a teacher and
her class as they go on field trips to historic sites from the Revolutionary War era.
ISBN 0-689-84004-7 (hardcover)
1. United States—Social life and customs—To 1775—Juvenile poetry.
2. United States—History—Colonial period, ca. 1600–1775—Juvenile poetry.
3. Children's poetry, American. [1. United States—Social life and customs—To 1775—Poetry.
2. United States—History—Colonial period, ca. 1600–1775—Poetry. 3. American poetry.]
I. Alley, R. W. (Robert W.), ill II. Title.
PS3561.A775R48 2004
811'.54—dc21   2002009771

THE COLONIAL GAZETTE 1d

CONTENTS

The Revolutionary Mrs. Brown

My favorite teacher loves whimmy diddles,
Spillikin, muddlers, and country fiddles.

She fills her pocket with pieces of eight,
Eats johnnycakes from a pewter plate,

Dresses in petticoat, cap, and gown—
She's the historical Mrs. Brown.

She likes to churn butter, plant Indian corn,
March with a musket and powder horn,

To drum *rat-ta-tatting*, up and down—
She's the colonial Mrs. Brown.

My class loves to travel with Mrs. Brown
To an eighteenth-century farm or town.

There we pump the bellows, stack the logs,
Turn the spit on the firedogs,

Try on breeches and powdered wig,
Learn how to spin a whirligig,

Or taste a spoonful of gooseberry fool,
Hundreds of years away from school.

9

Ann at the Churn

Up and down, up and down,
plunging the dasher up and down,
waiting for butter to form out of cream.

I love butter. Up and down.
"As soon as you hear a ploppy sound,
the butter's 'come,'" the lady says.

Up and down, up and down,
waiting to hear that ploppy sound.
Instead it's just a shloopy sound.

I think my arm is wearing down.
Shloop, shloop, shloop, shloop.
I want to shout. Up and down.

"Churn it faster!" the lady says.
Upanddown, upanddown,
and still there isn't a ploppy sound.

I hate butter. Up and down.
Oops, do I hear a ploppy sound?
At last, at last the butter's done!

But I'll still be churning, up and down,
tonight in my dreams, up and down,
cream into butter. Up   and   dooown.

Grace Dips a Candle

We're not using melted tallow
like they did three hundred years ago.
But the candles drip and cool,

                              drip and cool,
the same way they did then.

We hold sticks, each with a dangling cord
to dip in the iron kettle on the fire.
Kneel, dip, go to the end of the line.
"Mine's getting fatter." James blows on his wax.
"So are you," Raymond says.

Sarah swings her candle back and forth,
then pokes it. "Ouch!"
She peels wax off her fingertip.
"Hey, I've got a wax fingerprint!"
Kevin tries to make a wax nose.

But I hold my candle carefully,
pretending the wick is homespun hemp,
and the wax is bear's grease.
And one small flame is the only light
I'll have tonight in the woods' long dark.

Cobblestones

The cobblestones are pink, black, gray, and white.
They make a jigsaw puzzle of the street,

With pieces shaped like oysters,
Arrowheads, turtles, loaves of bread.

They ought to be called wobblestones;
My feet feel every step I take.

Heather hobbles. Sheldon nearly falls.
Only this plump pigeon doesn't mind,

Dancing on his sharp red toes
From stone to stone to stone to stone.

Colonial
GAZETTE
all the news
that fits in

13

What Did Colonial Kids Play?

Rolling hoops and flying kites,
Ice skating, bird-nesting, snowball fights.
Willow whistle, windmill, wooden top, popgun,
Bilbo catcher, Jacob's ladder—all were fun!
Cratch cradle, huzzlecap, corn husk doll,
Water wheel, hobby horse—that's not all.
Skittles, stool-ball, alphabet blocks,
Leap frog, scotch-hoppers, Jack-in-the-box,
Marbles, pickadill, blindman's buff,
Jackstones, Game of Graces—isn't that enough?

Wooden Horse

Log for a body, branch for a head,
the toy horse stands on broomstick legs.
"This horse is two hundred years old," a sign says.
"That's even older than Mrs. Brown," says Ann.

I click my tongue at the horse.
Once some kid climbed onto him
and pretended to gallop
through woods without a path or end.

"I wonder what this horse has seen," says Mrs. Brown.
"Soldiers with muskets," Raymond says.
"Maybe bears," Ann says.
"And Indians." Sheldon smiles.

The horse doesn't say anything.
He stands on the rough wooden floor,
with a fleece for his saddle
and hundreds of years for his road.

Signing the Declaration

"The pointy edge goes on the paper,"
the lady says, handing me a quill.

"Where do they get these feathers?" Ann asks.
"From inside your head," Raymond says.
But the lady says, "From geese."

"What kind of ink is this?" Ann asks.
"Vinegar, berry juice, and salt," the lady says.
James sniffs it. "It smells good."

When I try to write, the paper moves,
and Mrs. Brown holds it still.

"Oh, no!" Grace says. "I made a blot!"
The lady pours sandy stuff on the page.
"This is called pounce," she says.
"Wipe it off when it's dry."

I pretend I'm signing
the Declaration of Independence,
and I try to make a fancy squiggle
beneath my name like Benjamin Franklin did.
But the stupid quill scratches;
it's hard just to write *Sarah Davis*.

My squiggle turns into a blob of ink,
and I yell, "Hey, where's the pounce?"

"Here!" Kevin pounces on Grace.
"Stop that!" Grace yells.
"Hey, you poked me!" Kevin says.
"Just with the feather part," Grace says.

"Kevin's paper is blowing away!" shouts Ann,
and Kevin goes running after it.

I look at the smudge where my name should be.
I'm glad we use pencils at school.

17

Blacksmith Shop

Clang, clang! the anvil rings.
Inside the blacksmith shop, it's hot and smoky;
something stinks. Grace holds her nose.

As we crowd around the forge, the fire spits.
"Stay back! Stay back!" the blacksmith warns.
He holds an iron rod in the fire

until the end glows cherry red.
Then he pounds it with a hammer,
turns it and pounds, turns and pounds.

Raymond shoves himself in front.
"You look big and tough," the blacksmith says,
"so you can pump the bellows."

Raymond grunts, pushing the wooden handle
with both hands. The bellows wheeze,
and air hisses into the forge.

The smith stirs the flame with a poker.
"Watch out for sparks!" he says,
and Heather jumps away.

"Phew!" Raymond wipes his face. "Burning up."
The blacksmith looks at him.
"What are you going to be when you grow up?"

"NOT A BLACKSMITH!" Raymond says.

Ye olde
Village
Smithee

18

Iron
Puzzles
Try them!

19

20

Corn Planting

We face the east, and then we cup
earth in our left hands, hold it up
while the lady called Grandmother
says a prayer,
thanking Creator for Mother Earth
the same way the People did
thousands of years ago.

Working in pairs, we hoe the ground;
we shape the earth into a mound,
patting it down
and digging a trench around it,
preparing the brown earth for corn
the same way the People did
thousands of years ago.

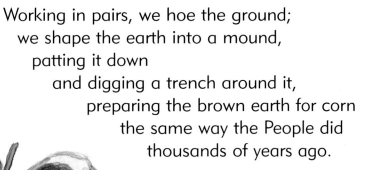

We place the seeds to spring forth
east, south, west, and north—
to honor Creator and Mother Earth,
the Sky Beings, and the creatures all,
planting the corn to grow tall
the same way the People did
thousands of years ago.

Shearing Poor George

A man holds George, the wether ram,
while another man shears.

They say George doesn't mind being sheared,
but he doesn't look happy to me.

When they clip near his head, he snorts,
and they cover his face with a hat.

George kicks his leg when he gets a chance.
The fleece comes off in a curly mound

like a cloud tumbling to earth.
When they finally let George up, he runs,

white hair jaggedy, pink showing through.
He's so skinny and funny looking,

I wish I could give him my sweater
until his own grows back.

Sarah Spins

The walking wheel turns slow,
the spindle fast.

The lady holds in her hand
a fuzzy clump of fleece,
which the spinning wheel
                                    draws out
into spun thread.

Stepping forward, stepping back,
she dances to the wheel's hum,

releasing the strand of woolen thread
that winds onto the spindle
and connects her to the wheel.

I'd like to spin the wheel myself,
so fast its hum would roar like the wind.
Would the spindle then whirrr
                                            into space,
carrying thread up to the clouds?

Would I be tied fast to the sky
by one thin strand of sheep?

Muster Drum

The drum is calling; we all line up.
Rat a tat tat RAT TAT
Breeches, kneesocks, buckles on shoes
Rat a tat TAT
Hatchets, pouches, powder horns, scythes
Rat a tat RAT
Hrrrrr hrrrrr dut dut dut dut

The sergeant yells to the beat of the drum.
Rat a tat tat RAT TAT
"Make ready!" *Ratata ratata*
"Pre-*sent*!" *Rat ta tat*
"Shoulder firelocks!" *Rat a TAT TAT*
"March!" *RAT TAT TAT*

PARADE GROUND

24

Shouldering sticks, we march in a row.
Rat a tat tat RAT TAT
Our line's crooked. *Rat a tat TAT*
The sergeant yells. *Rat a tat RAT*
"Stick together like chewing gum!"
Ratatat ratatat ratatat tat

James turns left instead of right.
Rat a tat tat RAT TAT
Kevin steps on Mrs. Brown's foot.
Rat a tat TAT
Sheldon trips and drops his stick.
Rat a tat RAT
Hrrrrr hrrrrr dut dut dut dut

Now the sergeant hoists his spontoon.
Rat a tat tat RAT TAT
"Stay in line!" *RAT a TAT*
"March to the charge!"
Rattata rattata rattata rattata
Everyone yells, "Huzzah!" *RAT TAT*

25

Indian Hemp

To turn this stick into rope,
we snap and pull it,
   snap again and pull again.
"Ooh, look," Grace says, "a little thread!"
"It looks like worm guts," Kevin says.

  We snap and pull until each red brown stick
    is four long strips.
     Then rub, scrub, pound
    till every bit of outer bark is gone.
    Kevin hits his thumb and yells.

    Knotting the ends together,
    we roll the strips—
      back and forth
    on our laps,
     forward to twist, backward to tighten.

      We're making cordage for nets, snares,
       for carrying bags,
        fishing lines,
       for lashing wigwams together.
       "I'll use mine to catch Grace," Kevin says.

Dream Catcher

Dream catcher,
    fashioned of sinew
and willow branch—
    hang in the darkness,
        hang on my wall.

Dream catcher,
    strung with brown beads
and feathers—
    capture my bad dreams,
        catch them all.

Bad dream,
    drawn to the spirit bead,
catch in this net—
    trapped until morning,
        burn up in the light.

Good dream,
    soft as a grouse feather,
pass through this net—
    come to me,
        speak to my heart in the night.

Kitchen Animals

"Here's a spider," the lady says,
and Heather screams.
But it isn't a real spider;
it's a frying pan with three legs
and a handle as long
as a baseball bat.

"These are firedogs," the lady says,
and Kevin barks.
But they aren't dalmatians;
they're iron props for the spit
the kids would turn
while the meat was roasting.

The crane isn't a waterbird;
it's a metal arm that swings
a huge black kettle over the fire.
The butterfly's a hinge,
and the piggin is a bucket,
not any kind of pig.

The animals I'd like to see
are the mice, *real* mice,
who'd nibble the bread, eat the candles.
And the cat, *real* cat, who used to curl
on this warm hearth and purr
so hard I can still hear it purring.

Oven

Sarah sticks her head in the square hole
on one side of the fireplace.
"That's the oven," the lady says.
"Inside it's as big as a double bed."

"How do you set the temperature?" Ann asks.
"You turn the knob, stupid," Raymond says.
"Where's the knob?" the lady asks.
Everyone looks. No knob.

"You build a fire inside," the lady says.
  "When the bricks get hot,
    you scrape the ashes into the fireplace,
    then stick the bread in the oven."

  The iron door lifts off and on.
  The lady shows Raymond how heavy it is.
  "Oof!" he says, and sets it down fast,
just missing Mrs. Brown's toe.

"You use a wooden peel," the lady says,
"to take the bread out of the oven."
"Our pizza guy uses one of those," Sarah says.
"Boy," says Ann, "Mom never cooked like this!"

James Eats Chomp

We got to pick what we wanted to eat,
Any kind of historical treat;
Mrs. Brown made it into a game,
Picking a food just by its name—
And I picked chomp.

I could have picked snickerdoodles instead,
Whitpot, suppawn, Sally Lunn bread,

Hush puppies, brown Betty, flummery, crowdy,
Pocket soup, syllabub, apple pandowdy—
But I picked chomp.

Sarah chose scuppernongs (those are grapes),
Heather picked cookies called ginger cakes,
Sheldon took pemmican (that's dried meat),
And Grace wanted suckets, a candied sweet,
But I picked chomp.

I never guessed that dragées were candy,
That jumbals were great and grunt tasted dandy;
No one told me that jack wax was sweet
And Indian pudding was really a treat,
So I picked chomp.

Salad's the one food I truly hate,
So why are these vegetables heaped on my plate?
Raw and juicy, spicy-hot,
Chopped-up vegetables—that's what I got
When I picked chomp.

Powwow

boom   boom   boom   boom

Native nations
        dancing in peace,
from Tuscarora to Navajo.
Heartbeat of Mother Earth,
        drumbeats pound—
here are voices the forests know.

Sweet grass and cedar,
        fringes and beads,
women moving stately and slow.
Meadow grass waving,
        chants rising high—
here are voices the wildflowers know.

Purple and red,
        orange and yellow,
kids like me wearing deerskin and feathers.
Flash of two redwings
        high in the sky—
here are voices the blackbirds know.

Gourd rattles
        and jingling bells
call us to join the circle dance.
Sage and tobacco,
        hush of the pine—
here are voices *I* want to know.

boom   boom   boom   boom

Wild Animals

I believe that the trees remember
Wolverines, catamounts, black bears, wolves,
A cougar's high, quavering scream,
The soft padding of lynx's paws.

Wolverines, catamounts, black bears, wolves.
Behind the log cabin, the woods are thick.
The soft padding of lynx's paws
Shivers the leaves, shivers me.

Behind the log cabin, the woods are thick.
A cougar's high, quavering scream
Shivers the leaves, shivers me.
I believe that the trees remember.

History

Mrs. Brown says we've gone back in time,
Hearing guinea hens squawk and steeple clocks chime,
Drinking fresh water drawn from a well,
Sniffing a firepit's smoky smell,
Admiring a gown of indigo blue,
Or tasting a spoonful of venison stew.
Hand me my notebook; where's my pen?
I'm ready to go back again!

Glossary

anvil: metal surface on which a blacksmith hammers and shapes hot iron

apple pandowdy: chopped apples baked in a crust

bellows: device used to pump air to build up a fire

bilbo catcher: a ball and cup attached to a stick, used in a catching game for one person

breeches: pants that end below the knee, worn with high socks

brown Betty: dessert made of apples and bread crumbs

butterfly hinges: hinges shaped like butterflies, often used on wooden cabinets

catamount: short for cat of the mountain, used as a name for the mountain lion

chomp: spicy salad of Welsh origin

churn: wooden container used for making butter

cobblestones: naturally rounded stones used to pave city streets

crane: hinged iron rod used to hang pots over a fire in the kitchen fireplace

cratch cradle: colonial name for the game of cat's cradle

crowdy: thick oatmeal

dasher: wooden paddle blade on a long handle, plunged vigorously up and down in a churn to turn cream into butter

dragées: sugar-coated nuts or fruits

firedogs: tall iron supports used in a fireplace to hold the rod, or spit, for roasting meat

firelock: gun using flint to create a spark that ignites the gunpowder

firepit: hole dug for an outdoor fire, often lined with stones

flint: very hard rock that sparks when struck by metal

flummery: sweetened berry juice thickened with cornstarch

forge: special fireplace where iron is heated for shaping

Game of Graces: game in which two players each use a wooden stick to toss a wooden ring back and forth

ginger cakes: cookie-sized cakes flavored with ginger

gooseberry fool: dessert made with pureed gooseberries and cream

gown: one-piece dress

grandmother: expression used in many Native nations to show respect for a female elder

grunt: dough filled with fruit

guinea hen: small hen with blackish, white-spotted feathers, often found on colonial farms

hemp: plant fiber used for making rope products

hush puppies: cornmeal balls fried with fish

huzzlecap: penny-pitching game

Indian hemp: plant also known as dogbane, whose inner bark can be used for making rope or string

Indian pudding: corn pudding with sugar and spices

indigo: popular bright blue dye, grown in the deep South

jack wax: maple syrup poured over snow

jackstones: colonial name for the game of jacks

Jacob's ladder: row of wooden blocks glued to a strip of ribbon tape, which can be manipulated so that the blocks appear to tumble down a ladder

johnnycake: baked cornmeal cake, originally named journeycake because it could be carried on a trip and reheated over a campfire

jumbal: small sugar cake

muddler: mixer consisting of a paddle blade on a wooden handle, spun by rubbing it back and forth between the palms

musket: infantry gun

Navajo: southwestern nation, also known as the Dineh, which means "people"

peel: flat wooden blade with a very long handle

pemmican: dried, shredded meat, often mixed with fruit or maple sugar

petticoat: long, full skirt

pewter: common material for dishes, made by combining tin with one or more other metals

pickadill: form of tag played in the snow

pieces of eight: silver dollar cut into eight pieces to make small change

piggin: small wooden pail with one strip of wood, longer than the others, that's used as a handle

pocket: large pouch, fastened separately around the waist because colonial clothing had no built-in pockets

pocket soup: dried mixture similar to bouillion

pounce: fine sand or ground-up cuttlebone used to dry ink

powder horn: container made from an animal's horn, used to carry gunpowder

powwow: Native American gathering that includes drumming, singing, and dancing

quill: a stiff, horny feather from a goose or turkey, sharpened to use for writing

redwing: North American blackbird with red patches on its wings

Sally Lunn: rich, sweet egg bread

scotch-hoppers: colonial name for the game of hopscotch

scuppernongs: native grapes

sinew: animal tendon, often used for sewing

skittles: bowling game

snickerdoodles: cinnamon cookies

spider: pot with legs so that hot coals can be heaped under it

spillikin: game similar to pick-up sticks

spindle: the part of a spinning wheel onto which the yarn is wound

spirit bead: center bead in a dream catcher net; attracts and traps bad dreams

spit: rod on which meat is impaled to be cooked over a fire

spontoon: spearlike blade on a pole, carried by a military commander so that his men can easily locate him

steeple clock: clock in church steeple, used by the whole town because individual clocks were rare and often inaccurate

stool-ball: an ancestor of croquet

suckets: candied lemon or orange peel

suppawn: thick porridge of Indian cornmeal and milk

syllabub: drink made of milk, cider, and sugar

tallow: the fat of sheep or cattle

tobacco: a sacred plant; the smoke of tobacco, sweet grass, cedar, and sage is used to purify a dance circle

Tuscarora: Iroquoian-speaking nation, which became the sixth member of the Iroquois League in 1722

venison: deer meat, a staple food of people native to the Eastern Woodlands

walking wheel: large spinning wheel operated by stepping back to pull the wool away as it twists into yarn, then stepping forward to let the yarn wind onto the spindle

wether ram: extra male sheep who acts as companion to the main ram in the flock

whimmy diddle: notched stick with a propeller blade that turns when a second stick is rubbed across the notches

whirligig: spinning toy made of a button or wooden circle on a string

whitpot: bread pudding with nutmeg and rosewater

wigwam: dwelling made of a pole frame lashed together and covered with bark

ALGONQUIN

Lake Huron

HURON

MALECITE

PETUN

Lake Ontario

St. Lawrence River

PASSAMAQUODDY

Lake Erie

Seneca   Cayuga   Onodaga   Mohawk
Oneida

MOHICAN   ABENAKI

MIAMI   ERIE   IROQUIS

MAHICAN

PENOBSCOT

MUNSEE

Susquehanna River

Hudson River

WAPPINGER   NIPMUC

MASSACHUSETTS

SHAWNEE

Ohio River

Connecticut River

POCUMTUC

Mountains

Potomac River

SUSQUEHANNITOCKE

Delaware River

Lenape

PEQUOT   WAMPANOAG
MOHEGAN   NARRAGANSETT

Appalachian   Mountains

CONESTOGA   DELAWARE

MANTAUK

CHOPTANK

PAMUNKEY

Atlantic Ocean

TUTELO   CHICKAHOMINY

MATTAPONI

POWHATAN

NANTICOCK

James River

TUSCARORA

NOTTAWAY

Roanoke River

SUGEREE

Cape Fear River

CHEROKEE   CATAWBA

PAMLICO

Savannah River

Santee River

WOCCON

ROANOKE

CREEK
Hitchiti
Yemasee
Appalachicola

Altamaha River

SEMINOLE

a MAP of NATIVE
TRIBES and NATIONS
of North America
showing also topographic features
indicated by their modern names